CANOPY

A Collection of Stories

Zakariyas James

Rumination Press

Copyright © 2026 Zakariyas James

All rights reserved. No part of this book may be reproduced, stored in a retrieval system, or transmitted in any form or by any means, electronic, mechanical, photocopying, recording, or otherwise, without the prior written permission of the author, except for brief quotations used in reviews or scholarly works.

ISBN: 979-8-218-93362-3

First Appearance Notice: "Seed" first appeared in *Tales of the Unknown* (The Writers Workout, 2025).

Disclaimer: This is a work of fiction. Any resemblance to actual persons, living or dead, events, or locales is purely coincidental.

Printed in the United States of America

For my wife and our son

TABLE OF CONTENTS

Seed 1

Root 13

Stem 25

Leaf...31

Author's Note

These stories began as observations. Watching the world, its patterns, its technologies, its quiet reshaping of human life, I asked: Where might this lead?

CANOPY is a record of those questions. It is a tracing of systems that influence, constrain, and define us, often before we even notice. Each story grows from something real: the surveillance of nature, the extension of memory into machines, the unseen decisions that ripple through society, the pressures shaping a child's world.

This collection is less about spectacle than consequence.

Across these four stories runs a shared observation: humans are endlessly creative, endlessly adaptive, and endlessly vulnerable. Structures, whether technological, bureaucratic, or social, do not merely govern. They shape the very perception of what is possible, what is right, and what is inevitable.

—Zakariyas James

Seed

It had been a while since Ulmus felt full after a late-night meal; longer still since he'd seen his wife Linnea eat everything on her plate. For months she had taken to scraping mouthfuls into the trash, whispering gleefully, "thin is in." As if she weren't already thin. As if everyone weren't.

The apartment offered little beyond its walls: pale concrete, a pair of chairs older than Ulmus, and the hollow echo of their breathing. Even the air seemed empty as their stomachs.

Across the zone, it was the same. Perhaps across the entire State, though neither of them could imagine traveling far enough to know. Citizens survived on the ration cycle: sealed packets of powdered meals, a few nicotine pouches, and—if they cared to know—scraps of gossip about strangers they would never meet. Travel was not forbidden, but exhaustion made it impossible. The outside existed only in memory, rumor, and the curated images on monitors.

Every morning, the soft chime of their wristbands reminded them of the state-mandated meal schedule. Ulmus's gaze fell on the cold, smooth surface of his device. A blinking red icon warned: Nicotine level low. Please consume within 30 minutes to maintain compliance. His thumb hovered, then slid reluctantly. The faint vibration reassured him—the system was watching.

Linnea's band buzzed too, a soft pulse beneath her pale skin. She barely noticed. Years of constant monitoring—vitals, consumption, all fed directly to the State's health network—rendered resistance unthinkable. Any deviation invited scrutiny. Any excess, punishment.

The next morning unfolded as always, with a growl in Ulmus's stomach and Linnea repeating the phrases plastered across every building: "The past is putrid. The present, pristine. The past is putrid. The present, pristine."

"Ulmus, how come it's so hard for you to say it with me?" she asked, scrubbing the same patch of floor for the fourth time.

"I do it in my head with you," he said finally, deciding to lie. Linnea paused only briefly before resuming her fevered motion.

"Well, if that's the best you can do, you might as well clean too," she quipped.

The silence shattered as a siren blared outside their frail home, a mechanical voice repeating the State's mantra: "A leaner world is a cleaner world."

Linnea shifted her mantra entirely, scrubbing harder, desperate to prove her obedience.

Ulmus watched her and wondered if freedom had ever truly existed. Did it look anything like this? Would he even recognize it? His father had told wild stories of places and things Ulmus was certain no longer existed; perhaps they never had, and his father simply had a gift for storytelling. Either way, Ulmus could not summon enough clarity to imagine much at all—freedom, life outside the city, or even the taste of something called Texas meatloaf.

Morning arrived with the sting of bleach, heavy in the air where the State sprayed the walls and streets. Linnea was the first to leave, her wristband pulsed insistently, summoning her to her daily assignment. Ulmus remained slumped, as though staying low might shield him from the biting fumes. The pale grey of her State-issued uniform swallowed her figure as she slipped into the hallway, her whispered mantras trailing behind like a ghost.

Outside, the city shuffled silently. Linnea blended into the column of workers, her steps brisker than most, as though eagerness could disguise her weakness.

Near the corner where concrete met a strip of sandy loam, something stirred. A woman bent so suddenly, the line of bodies faltered around her. Her hand scraped the ground, fingers trembling, and when she rose, a thin worm flailed in her grasp.

Her eyes widened, alive with a hunger so deep it was almost luminous. Ancient. She raised it toward her mouth, jaw quivering, lips parting. The sight was obscene not because it was filthy, but because it was honest.

Sirens shrieked from the nearest patrol drone. The crowd recoiled, but the woman did not. Even as the officers closed in, even as their hands clamped down and wrenched her arms behind her back, her eyes stayed fixed on the worm.

It fell, twisting, onto the pavement. She strained against the hold, not to escape, not to plead, but to watch it wriggle away. Her hunger was unrelenting, her body shaking not with fear but with loss.

When the officers forced her to the ground, pressing her face into the concrete, she did not cry out. She did not resist. With her cheek against the ground, she realized she'd taste the worm if she licked the spot where it had fallen. Her gaze never wavered, her breath hitching as it slipped into a crack in the street and vanished from sight.

The punishment meant nothing. The humiliation meant nothing. What broke her was the absence, the empty space where her meal had been.

The crowd shuffled faster, heads bowed, as though erasing her could erase the gnawing in their own stomachs.

Linnea's heart thudded—not with fear, but indignation. How dare the woman jeopardize the order everyone else had worked so hard to preserve? Linnea quickened her pace, whispering under her breath with renewed conviction: a cleaner world…

That evening, she recounted the scene to Ulmus, eyes bright with the energy she rarely showed anymore.

"You should've seen her, Ulmus. Snatching it up like some filthy animal, as if she were entitled to nature itself," she said, voice sharp with pride. "I swear, if the officers hadn't gotten there first, I would've dragged her down myself. People like that—they don't deserve to be among us. They're a disease."

Ulmus sat silent, stomach knotted tighter than hunger alone could explain. He studied Linnea as she spoke, her face alight not with compassion or fear, but devotion to the system. In that moment, he realized that whatever remained of his wife, the woman he once knew, was being scraped away.

That evening, the apartment was dim except for the faint glow of the InPhant in Linnea's lap. She cradled it as if it were fragile, though its surface was smooth and indestructible. Its too-perfect eyes blinked in even intervals, a rhythm designed to soothe.

"Mama, I missed you," it chimed, the voice pitched just high enough to mimic innocence.

Linnea's lips curved, tender in a way Ulmus hadn't seen directed at him in years. "I missed you too," she whispered, brushing its cheek with her thumb. "Did you behave today?"

Her voice softened, filling with warmth. Each touch, each button press triggered a pre-programmed sigh of contentment from the device. Ulmus sat across the room, watching as the machine rewarded her with glow and chirp, glow and chirp. Each netted a measure of satisfaction.

It reminded him of the woman on the street, her eyes fixed on the worm with the ferocity of real hunger. Linnea's gaze mirrored that same desperation, but it was aimed at nothing alive. Where the woman had strained against officers for a single wriggling scrap of life, Linnea poured her longing into plastic and circuitry.

The InPhant was full where she was empty.

Ulmus's stomach tightened. Whatever tenderness Linnea had once given freely had been rerouted, siphoned away by something manufactured. She hummed as she fed it phantom meals, stroked it, praised it. Her hunger was quieted not by food, but by the illusion of giving.

"I gave you an extra portion of attention today," she said proudly, pressing the praise button. The InPhant's eyes brightened, chirping in elongated delight.

Ulmus clenched his hands, thinking of the worm slipping into the crack in the pavement, and the woman's empty stare as it vanished. That hunger was honest. This glowing imitation was worse.

The next morning, the city screens bloomed to life. Forests swaying in sunlight, rivers flashing silver, hills rolling endless and green. Each was labeled in clean white script: Corridor 1. Corridor 2. Corridor 3. Citizens slowed in their steps, not out of wonder but obedience, faces tilted upward in practiced attention. A calm voice narrated the State's devotion to preservation, its promise to protect what was left.

Linnea stopped. Her lips parted, and for a moment she looked younger, softened by awe. "Look, Ulmus. See what they've done? Beautiful, isn't it? They protected it all for us. They care so much."

Ulmus didn't answer. He kept walking, though his eyes dragged back to the images. Too vivid. Too perfect. A certainty gnawed at him: these corridors were curated illusions, staged and sealed, never to be touched by hands like his. No one he knew had ever been assigned to such places. For all he knew, they didn't exist at all.

At the factory, his wristband pulsed: Nicotine low. Calories low. Productivity optimal. He tapped confirmation without thought, the gesture as unconscious as breathing. Around him, men and women moved in silence, bodies locked into rhythm with the machines.

Then a sound broke the monotony—sharp, flat, unmistakable. A coworker's wristband. Ulmus had heard it before. The man blinked once, then was puffed off the line as he requested more nicotine pouches. His body still functioned, but the data no longer justified the cost of keeping it alive.

Linnea would have approved. It isn't cruelty, she would have told him later, gentle but firm. It's efficiency.

That night, Ulmus's body betrayed him. A tear slipped down his cheek before he could stop it, hot and useless. Not for the man—he'd seen that before—but for something he could not name. He quickly wiped it, ashamed. In a world that measured every breath, even tears felt like theft. Misuse of water.

Mundane weeks blurred past in choreographed repetition before anything shifted. On the morning commute, Ulmus noticed an older man keeping pace a few steps behind. His gait was uneven, his frame thinned almost to breaking, yet somehow he moved with intent.

At the next turn, the man drew closer, slipping into step beside him. His face was lined, his eyes carrying the kind of depth Ulmus had only ever seen in people close to dying.

"You've gotten older," the man murmured, so softly Ulmus wasn't sure the words were real. "You look like your father."

Ulmus froze inside, though his body kept walking. He had learned not to react too quickly to anything unusual, it was safer that way.

The man's hand brushed his, rough and urgent. Something small and hard was pressed into Ulmus's palm before their fingers parted. The grip lingered a moment too long, as if to pin the object there, to make sure it could not be dropped.

"Don't look at it here," the man whispered. His voice was cracked but steady. "Wait until you're home."

Ulmus's pulse hammered. He wanted to look, wanted to know, but he didn't dare. The crowd pressed forward in its usual shuffle, oblivious. The man peeled away, blending back into the bodies as if he had never been there.

Ulmus walked the rest of the way with his hand buried in his coat pocket, the small object grinding against his fingers through the fabric. It was nothing, he told himself. A stone, a bead, a trick. Still, the weight of it seemed to grow heavier with every step, as though it carried more than itself.

By the time he reached his station, his palm ached from pressing it too hard, as if pain might reveal what it was. He kept his hand clenched, keeping the secret intact. He didn't know why, only that it mattered.

That evening, Linnea fussed over her InPhant again, humming as if its chirps were music. Ulmus's stomach clenched. His thoughts kept circling back to the object burning a hole in his pocket. He hadn't even seen it, yet thoughts of it consumed him. Should he wait until she slept, or risk pulling it out now?

Linnea paused mid-story, recounting the worm incident to her digital dependent as though it were a parable of virtue. The InPhant blinked, chirped, rewarded her pride.

Ulmus's hand slid into his pocket. For the first time that day, he focused on the details of the object instead of the danger it invited. Small. Rounded, but imperfect. He rolled it between thumb and forefinger, feeling the faint ridges. Every nerve screamed to know what it was. Every fear warned him not to find out.

Linnea once might have shared his curiosity. That Linnea was gone. This one was devoted to her surrogate child, her slogans, her obedience.

He pressed the thing harder between his fingers. Then, before he could second-guess himself, he drew it into the light.

A seed.

The word itself filled his head like contraband. His father had whispered about them, only in shadows, only in the tone one used for sin. To hold one was to commit treason. To see one was unthinkable. And yet, here it was, the smallest thing Ulmus had ever possessed, and the heaviest.

His breath caught. Panic overtook him; he shoved it back into his pocket before Linnea could glance up. The InPhant chirped, its glow painting her face in soft delight. She cooed at it, blind to the terror seated across from her.

Possession of seeds was forbidden. Everyone knew. They belonged only to the State, relics of a world too unruly, too wasteful, too alive. Life, the announcements insisted, must be measured.

Cultivated. Controlled. Cut short, if need be.

His hand shook against his thigh. He thought of discarding it by dropping it into the waste chute with the day's scraps, erasing the danger before it erased him. But the object pulsed heavier each moment, as though it had a heartbeat.

Should I show her? The thought pressed down on him, thicker than hunger. But then he imagined her eyes narrowing, her thumb flicking across the report button on her wristband. Officers pounding the door. The Linnea who once had questions for him only in the safety of the dark was gone. This Linnea was loyal; engineered in spirit if not in flesh.

He told himself to wait. To bury it. To never let her see.

But then she laughed, telling the worm story again to her InPhant, smiling as if starvation itself were proof of righteousness.

Something inside Ulmus tore. He could not stand her joy in a sterilized world, a world where children were manufactured illusions and dirt was worth more than human life.

His hand moved on its own. Slowly, deliberately, he placed the seed on the table.

"I have to show you something, Linnea," he whispered. His voice cracked. "It's not pristine. But it's not putrid either."

Linnea froze. Her eyes widened. Her thumb hovered over the wristband, a single twitch away from summoning officers.

The apartment fell silent, save for the hum of the city and the sirens outside chanting their nightly refrain: A leaner world is a cleaner world.

Ulmus's heart pounded. The seed sat between them, motionless, defiant. A fragment of truth in a room built on obedience.

"What is that?" Linnea asked, voice sharp, almost mechanical. She set the InPhant aside, covering its screen as if shielding it—or shielding them from its ears. Her gaze rose slowly from the seed to Ulmus's eyes.

"It's a seed," he whispered. "I think. I'm sure."

Her breath quickened. Her wristband chirped a warning, detecting strain. Just as her lips parted, the InPhant erupted—a piercing, sustained shriek. Both of them clutched their ears. Their wristbands blared commands: Rest. Comply. Consume nicotine.

Then silence.

The InPhant's eyes glowed red. Its voice rang flat, metallic, final:

"Unauthorized object detected. Unauthorized object detected."

Root

The gentlest light of dawn, reaching through spruces and hemlocks, showcased mist enveloping the forest floor and a single Corridor attendant carefully treading over moss. The branches brushed against his sleeves, never snagging as he was mindful of his impact. Though called the wild, the trees seemingly welcomed his passage with warbler calls and a breeze from behind that ushered him in deeper. In the fractions of silence, the weight of the aromatic depth would almost overwhelm the attendant.

Each breath provided insight on the richness of the soil, the potency of pollen on the wind, the water in a creek some yards away. The magnitude of difference between this environment and the sterility of the State's dwelling zones ceaselessly amazed and humbled him.
He checked his equipment, as instructed. Compared the readings to the meters grafted onto the trees by the State. All seemed balanced. Just like last time.

He repeated his truth: The Corridor is sacred. Pristine.

He was trained to take a new path each visit to not leave even the smallest trace of his existence. No memory. As he snaked his way through, time bent. He could not say if it was minutes or hours, only that the Corridor pulled him deeper, the trance of leaves dancing carrying him forward.

The expanse seemed endless. Each step disrupted sedges and rush, but quickly erased by the grasses standing back up. As though the Corridor itself wanted him to vanish. Amidst the variety of sounds, mostly the leaves dropping and the birds calling, the only constant he expected was the rhythm of his breathing. He felt nearly absorbed by it all but he knew he wasn't part of the forest at all.

Then—movement.

Not the jitter of a squirrel, nor the startle of a deer. This was upright, steady. His body froze before his mind caught up. Through layers of spruce and shadow, a shape separated itself from the trunks. Human.

The posture alone confirmed it, though the stride was also too measured to belong to any beast. For a moment, the figure was only a silhouette among the trees, blackened by distance. As the light shifted, a striking fabric unlike any pelt he'd ever seen: elaborate folds, a gleam of lace, the piercing flash of polished button. Clothing so out of place in the sanctity of the Corridor that it sickened him.

His jaw tightened, anger shoving aside the shock. What arrogance—to step here, dressed like that, as though this place was a theater. He clenched his fists until his knuckles burned, stomach coiling with fury and fear.

The figure moved again, drifting deeper into the woods. No sound followed it. No snap of twig, no crunch of leaf. Silent—as though the woods itself permitted its passage.

He held his breath, waiting for the illusion to fracture. A trick of the light, he told himself. A figment. But each blink returned the same truth: the figure persisted, stubborn. Then the mist condensed, seemingly choosing to erase it.

His pulse hammered, loud enough he thought it might shake the leaves.

The Corridor was supposed to be sacred. Untouched.

So what had he just seen?

The attendant recounted the sighting, describing every detail—the posture, the fabric, the buttons.

His supervisor leaned back, fingers crossed, eyes narrowing. "You've been under stress," he said carefully. "Excessive exposure to the Corridor can cause…illusions. A few of the species you may come across have psychoactive compounds, so it's likely your wristband monitor is faulty and didn't notice you were under some influence. You should put in a work order."

The supervisor's lips curved faintly, almost imperceptibly, as if amused by knowledge the attendant could not see.

The attendant swallowed, insistence bubbling in his chest. "But I—"

"You've been imagining things," the supervisor cut in smoothly, though a flicker in his eyes conveyed something else. "There was nothing there that required intervention. Take a medical evaluation. Put in the work order. Rest. The root of the problem is your mental state. Report only confirmed readings moving forward."

The supervisors cane tapped lightly against the table leg. "Do not invent stories to impress us. Your mind can betray you. Be vigilant—of yourself."

So he left, mind racing. Every instinct told him the figure had been real, yet the authority of the supervisor denied even its possibility. The Corridor's silence now mirrored the supervisor's words: erasure, denial, control.

After his mandated rest period, he was summoned back to his duties in the Corridor. He was terrified of finding the nameless intruder—but equally terrified of finding nothing. Had he really seen what he thought he saw? Could it have been a hallucination his supervisor so confidently named? His fists, tightened for days now, loosened only when he stepped beneath the boughs again.

He checked his equipment, scanning for predators. Safety verified, he set forth with one goal not given by the State: find even the faintest trace of the ghost that haunted him.

He bounded through a stand of birch, blind to the kudzu strangling their trunks this far north—a growth he would ordinarily flag for immediate culling. The sedge and rush resisted his stride, tangling his boots, urging patience. His body demanded speed but failed him, forcing an extended pause among a patch of asters. Chickadees broke into sudden song above, as if mocking his impatience.

His wristband pulsed: heart rate elevated, pause activity.

"Well, at least that works," he muttered. He slowed, obeyed the order, forced breath into rhythm. The grasses seemed thinner once he conceded.

Then—something foreign. A sharp fragrance, abominable among the usual catalog of smells. Smoke. His eyes stung before he could convince himself it was imagined. No alerts registered on his equipment—no fire detected. He closed his eyes, nose tilted upward, tracking the phantom column. But the breeze betrayed him. He opened them again with a grim smile. I'm not a dog.

Adjusting course, he followed potency instead of sight. Near a lone aspen, the sting in his sinuses intensified, verified by a fit of sneezes. Equipment readings: nothing. His scowl deepened. He stowed the tool—and as he twisted, he caught it. A faint, pale wisp rising from the moss at his feet.

He crouched. In the greenery lay a small, glowing stub. A cigarette.

The smell, the sting, the proof—consolidated into a fragile, discarded tube. He snatched it up, heat searing into his palm. For the first time since the sighting, he felt relief in pain. Vindication. He had not hallucinated. His wristband had not failed. His supervisor was wrong.

There was someone here. Now.

He surged upright, spinning on his heel, eyes combing the treeline. Nothing belonging to the forest could claim this waste. Only a human. Only a violator.

He crushed the butt in his fist, savoring the burn as it pressed into his skin. The Corridor was sacred. He had proof that someone dared to desecrate, to trespass.

He prayed—actually prayed—that they had left more trash. Enough to follow. Enough to lead him straight to them. The thought horrified him though. For a brief moment, he wanted something in the Corridor to not be pristine.

Reeling from his own ideations, the attendant fell to his knees. I'm here to protect this place, not to beg for trash.

The woods hushed at his confession. Leaves stilled, birds mute. Then, as if to encourage him, a gust of wind pressed firmly at his back. He steeled himself, rising like the smoke. Determined to find the culprit, relay the coordinates to headquarters, and fulfill his duty, he set his jaw. The trees seemed to wait, every branch angled forward, goading him deeper.

He pressed forward, the path narrowing into a slow funnel of birch and pine. Strides felt louder, the moss less forgiving, the branches creaking and groaning overhead. His eyes swept, hungry for another sign.

It came suddenly, half-hidden among the branches of a low spruce.

Lace.

A torn fragment, pale as bone, snagged on a needle. Its delicacy struck him harder than the cigarette had—fabric made not for labor or survival, but ornament. It fluttered faintly in the draft. Fragile, obscene. He reached for it with trembling fingers. The thread caught against his skin, soft. It belonged to someone alive, someone who had passed through here.

His jaw locked. This was no hallucination. This was intrusion.

Yet as he turned the scrap over in his palm, his chest strained from a strange, unbidden awareness: the lace was beautiful. Impossibly delicate. It seemed to hum against his skin, as though the environment itself conspired to keep it from fraying.

He shoved it into his pocket, hands trembling, muttering the only words that gave him ground: The Corridor is sacred. Pristine.

But with every step he took, the lace in his pocket proved him wrong.

It burned against his thigh with every step back to the checkpoint. He told himself it was evidence, nothing more—but the truth clung to him. Its softness, its strange perfume of old fabric and sweat. Each time he touched it through his pocket, he felt a shiver that was both shame and thrill. He would keep that secret. For now.

But the cigarette—that would prove him right. That would silence the supervisor's accusations of madness.

He entered the sterile chamber, the sudden absence of natural smells replaced by the jolt of disinfectant gave him focus. His supervisor sat rigidly at his desk, ledger open, as though already expecting failure. The attendant stepped forward and with a trembling hand, placed the cigarette butt on the polished wood.

The supervisor's reaction was instant—not alarm, not recognition, but rage. The cane came down so fast it felt rehearsed. The glint in his eyes revealed the truth: he enjoyed it. The shock split through the younger man's body; the butt rolled, leaving a smear of ash on the immaculate surface.

"You dare tarnish my desk?" the supervisor barked. He snatched up the stub with two fingers, holding it away from himself like refuse. "Filth. Have you no discipline?"

The attendant clutched his hand, stunned. "It was in the Corridor," he managed, breath ragged. "Still burning. Someone left it there. I—"

"Silence." The supervisor dropped the butt into a dish, as though disposing of vermin. "This object is no proof of anything except your clumsiness. Cigarettes have been banned by the State for decades. They take years to degrade. Years. Occasionally old trash resurfaces when the moss shifts." His voice tightened on the last word, savoring it like a moral victory.

The attendant blinked, throat dry. "But—it was lit. The smoke…"

"Do not contradict me," the supervisor hissed, tapping the cane against the desk with composed rhythm. He leaned back slightly, gaze fixed, lips curved—not into a snarl, but something quieter. Satisfaction. He liked making the younger man flinch.

The attendant lowered his gaze, confusion knotted in his chest. He had smelled it. He had held the heat in his palm. And yet the supervisor's words landed heavy, authoritative, inescapable.

The lace in his pocket seemed even more dangerous, a hidden truth he could not share.

Days later, the attendant was summoned to courier duty within the administrative wing. He loathed the place. Sterile halls, the ventilation's dull hiss, a faint sting of bleach—but he obeyed.
His route carried him through one of the exhibition corridors, where the State displayed its sanctioned collection: oil paintings seized or salvaged from collapsed cultures. A wall of warning. Kings and nobles,

colonies and courts—figures dressed in fabrics too extravagant to excuse.

He had never cared to look at the paintings before. But now his eyes dragged themselves canvas to canvas, unwilling to release him.

And then—he stopped.

One painting showed a group standing on the edge of a monoculture clearing: men in tailored coats with gleaming buttons, women with lace collars and jeweled brooches. Their posture was exact, their clothing alien, yet familiar. His chest tightened. He had seen them. Not in paint. In the woods.

The breath drained from him. The lace in his pocket felt heavier than ever.

"I've seen this before," he whispered.

The supervisor turned with impatience. "Of course you have. You've had this work detail before." His cane ticked once against the marble floor. The clerks stifled thin smiles.

The attendant's mouth dried. He glanced toward the painting again, desperate for someone else to see. But the group's eyes—painted centuries ago—seemed fixed only on him. Watching. Waiting.

"Keep pace," the supervisor said flatly, already moving on.

When he returned to the Corridor, nothing felt the same. Birch bark glowed with unnatural sheen. Shadows bent longer than they should. Birdsong cracked the air like splintering glass. Even the grass moved with strange deliberation, slowing time around his steps.

The wind shifted unnaturally, carrying a heavy, predatory musk that made the hairs on his neck rise. He checked his equipment but saw nothing, though this didn't settle his sense of unease.

Every sense pressed harder on him. Colors richer. Air heavier. Silence deeper.

This place was no longer a sanctuary. It was a stage.

And he was no longer its guardian, but its audience.

He moved through thickets with senses stretched taut. He had become a predator in training, but still prey to what he saw. Then—her. Alone, framed by a shaft of morning light that turned every leaf to liquid gold, she stood as though the trees had waited for her. Her eyes locked onto his, unflinching. Challenging.

She began to undress. Each motion was willful, choreographed to ensnare. Buttons caught the light and slipped away; laces floated off in arcs. The garments that once marked her as intruder fell back, revealing skin unscarred and vibrant. His chest tightened, smoldering in a way he had never known—raw, insistent lust.

Desire waged war on discipline. He wanted to rush, to seize her, enforce the rules—but his body betrayed him. Every nerve ended in her. The tension was more than physical: it shredded the foundation of his training, forcing him to balance reverence and obsession, duty and forbidden longing.

The curve of her waist, the hypnotic rise of her chest demanded his gaze. She ran her hands along herself, mocking his restraint. His mind frayed, torn between awe and something raw, illicit, dangerous.

The grove itself seemed complicit, swaying with her. Light caressed the sweat at her collarbone. Time thickened; his pulse surged, vibrating through the mossy floor. He should look away. Retreat. Reassert control. But he could not.

She sensed it, gracefully closing the distance. Each step teased him further, stoking the fire in his chest. He imagined touching her, claiming her—his concern about her presence in the Corridor faded. He was lost entirely.

A faint smirk played across her lips. He realized with horror and rapture: she could see the war inside him. She slowly turned in place, drawing out the spectacle, each movement shattering him into desire and obedience simultaneously. He blinked, attempting to break the spell—but then: a twig snapped.

The whisper of movement made his blood run cold. The trap had sprung.

From the periphery, two men surrounded him like jaws. One struck with animalistic fury, driving him to the ground, punishing every movement, every gasp. The second moved like a surgeon, precise, cruel, ensuring every joint screamed in pain.

He tried to rise, to run, to do anything—but an exposed root on the surface grasped his foot, holding him in place. Stuck, his body betrayed him. Desire and shame twisted into pain.

She watched. Still, silent. Only her eyes and her smile moved. They burned into him as she recorded every shudder, every twitch, every surrender of his flesh and mind. She was the lure, the specter, now the voyeur of his death.

The forest itself seemed complicit. Damaged mosses echoed his flailing, branches slapped his shoulders. The earth smelled of blood and her faint perfume, mixing into a haze.

Pain became his only reality. Lust and horror crashed together, leaving him fragmented. The winds carried the echo of his cries, yet the trees remained indifferent. The only movement was his writhing.

The blows stopped. Silence pressed in, broken only by the rasp of his ruined breath. He tried to lift his head, to hold her in his vision one last time, but the forest had already reclaimed her. She was gone.

From the treeline, a shadow moved. A low growl announced the arrival of a predator. It did not attack in fury, but in function—methodical, precise, as though summoned by the forest itself. Teeth closed over what remained, dragging him deeper into the green.

The Corridor exhaled. Moss knitted back together erasing his impression, branches bent back into place. By the time the predator disappeared, nothing remained but light and birdsong.

To any attendant who followed, the Corridor would appear untouched, sacrosanct, eternal.

Somewhere beyond sight, the supervisor allowed himself a small smile. The illusion endured.

Stem

"Let's dispense with the language of transition," he said evenly. "What we're discussing now is stabilization."

The room recalibrated around the sentence. Any residual doubt—procedural, moral, or strategic—collapsed under the weight of its framing. Around the table sat principals with assistants positioned just behind them, quiet figures moving in and out of relevance, passing folded briefs, murmuring updates that never interrupted the flow but subtly altered posture, pacing, emphasis. Things were happening elsewhere.

The Architect stood at the head of the table, eyes fixed on a projection that showed no totals, only relationships; trends without quantities, dependencies without names.
"Continuity is a stem," he added, almost conversationally, "from which permissible behaviors branch."

The Environmental Systems lead spoke first, after an assistant slipped a thin document into his hand.

"Corridor implementation assumes permanent human exclusion. Are we proceeding with symbolic preservation, or functional isolation?"

"Isolation is the function," the Architect replied. "Symbolism follows once access is removed."

The assistant behind Environmental Systems made a note that did not look provisional.

The Public Health director leaned forward as a whisper reached his ear, then spoke without acknowledging it.

"If restriction stabilizes behavior initially, what prevents long-term cognitive fatigue from degrading compliance?"

"Fatigue precedes equilibrium," the Architect said. "Dependency substitutes absorb the transition. Unbounded access to goods reinforces destabilizing patterns of mind."

No one challenged the premise.

The Treasury representative did not look down when his assistant placed a paper beside him.

"If accumulation is deprecated," he asked, "what replaces equity as the stabilizing signal? What does the individual balance sheet resolve to when ownership is removed but participation must still compound?"

"Participation becomes legible," the Architect said. "Visibility replaces possession. Once alignment is measurable, deviation becomes expensive without intervention."

No one dared to clarify why the word measurable was used or what it entails.

The Security head spoke next, after a brief murmur at his shoulder.
"When access is reduced, how do we ensure the outcome resolves as individual failure rather than coordinated restriction?"

"By flooding attribution," the Architect replied. "No single explanation, only repetition. With enough instances and unique explanations, responsibility disperses. The individual selects the one that indicts them."

The assistant behind Security adjusted a document on the table, as if to gently bring it to attention.
The Ethics liaison waited. His assistant said nothing.
"If behavior is shaped without explicit coercion," he asked, "what governs the boundary between guidance and compulsion?"

He paused, then continued carefully. "And when a minority insists on naming the outcome as harm—rejecting the framework, resisting its language—how is that dissent contained without elevating it into a moral counterweight?"

"It isn't elevated," the Architect said. "It's reclassified."

The liaison's eyes narrowed slightly, not from objection. A cue that clarification was needed here.

"Persistent non-alignment presents first as linguistic instability," the Architect continued. "From there it resolves clinically. Stress disorders. Adjustment delays. Perceptual fixation. All treatable."

"Voluntarily?" the Ethics liaison asked.

"Compliance improves markedly once distress is addressed," the Architect said. "Stability is the highest form of compassion."

The assistant behind Ethics cautiously looked around the room to gauge reactions, though no one else dared to do the same.

The Treasury representative spoke again, shorter this time.
"Understandably, due to the hyperfractionalization of assets over the last five years driven by liquidity stress, most participants hold marginal exposure. At best, their holdings are low-impact. How does the continuity model convert this into a credible equity signal once accumulation no longer clears behavior?"
"By decoupling equity from possession," the Architect replied. "Access tiers replace title. Eligibility compounds. Value should serve survival and community coherence, not personal vanity."

The Public Health director returned, quieter now.
"When deprivation is reframed as misalignment, what prevents despair from externalizing?"

"Submission scales faster than resistance," the Architect said. "Once a critical mass adopts the language, enforcement migrates downward. Communities correct tone. Institutions withdraw."

The room felt narrower. Not tense, but resolved. Papers shifted. One assistant seemed frozen, probably focusing on hiding their gut reactions for some time now.

The Ethics liaison spoke once more.
"At what point does alignment cease to be voluntary if eligibility becomes the only remaining form of equity—and is that threshold explicit or implicit?"

"Implicit systems persist longer," the Architect said.

Treasury asked the final question, without emphasis.
"And when conditional inclusion is eventually discounted—what absorbs the loss?"

The Architect did not look up.
"The system does not carry non-performing variables."

No one spoke after that. No one needed to.

Leaf

Ulmus was seven when his father realized the arguments had ended. Not just publicly. Not officially. But at the level where arguments used to live. Kitchens, classrooms, the space between a question and an answer no longer experienced rebuttal or retraction. The world still looked intact enough to debate language instead of survival, which allowed most people to ignore what was happening or miss it altogether.

The change was gentle. School notices began to speak less about learning and more about alignment. Health advisories used words like stable and community-created. The signs at bus stops and clinics softened their edges. Because nothing was actually forbidden. Nothing was named as permanent. Everything was provisional in tone, while absolute in implication.

Ulmus came home one afternoon and repeated a phrase he started hearing at school, with a slight error. His father corrected him without thinking; he didn't agree with the statement but he knew the correct phrasing and now he felt a weight.

Not because the phrase mattered, but because the act of correcting it did. He realized, with a sudden clarity that made him sit down, that speech was becoming infrastructure, and that his family was not immune to the changes he's been seeing.

From that day forward, he listened differently, to others and to his son.

What followed did not resemble persuasion. Persuasion requires alternatives. This was presented as coordination. Precision language. Harm-minimizing vocabulary. Teachers received updated guidance, parents received emails offering support for linguistic alignment. Some words began producing reactions instead of arguments—pauses in conversation, a shift in tone, an instinctive single-step retreat while speaking.

Adults began waiting longer before speaking. That the last person to speak was often the one closest to authority. Disagreement did not disappear; it compressed. It learned to pass unnoticed.

Ulmus's father considered explaining this to his son. He rehearsed sentences in his head that named the manipulation clearly and cleanly. Each version sounded like a burden being placed where it did not belong. Why should a child be taught how to safely toe a line he did not yet know existed?

So he chose something harder.

"Listen before you repeat," he told his son.

"Notice who speaks last."

"Pay attention to what makes adults nervous."

He did not teach defiance. He taught pattern recognition. He taught his son how to see without announcing what he saw.

At night, after Ulmus slept, his father lay awake and measured his own restraint. Each withheld explanation felt like a small betrayal. He was supposed to be his son's best teacher, his guide to the world. But each explanation withheld preserved something fragile. He began to understand that protection did not always look like resistance. Sometimes it looked like absorption. Sometimes it looked like preservation.

Preservation, once instinctive, began to require method.

The shortages did not arrive as a collapse. They arrived as delays, subtle enough to feel temporary, familiar enough to be tolerated. Mining suspensions were announced under environmental necessity, followed closely by repurposing mandates. Nothing new, only reclaimed. The logic was elegant, almost comforting in its restraint, and the execution quiet enough that most people experienced it only as a change in rhythm rather than a loss. Manufacturing did not fail in any way that demanded attention; it thinned. Devices lasted longer because they had to. Infrastructure projects stalled without ceremony. Data centers learned to breathe more slowly. Currency continued to circulate, and because daily life remained mostly intact, the bans gathered praise instead of resistance.

People adapted before they were asked to.

Conversations shifted. Excess became something discussed with mild embarrassment. Durability was praised. Replacement felt indulgent. People began telling stories about how little they needed, not because anyone required it, but because restraint now carried a social weight that abundance no longer did.

Ulmus noticed the changes before he understood them. Certain toys stopped appearing in store windows. Repairs took longer. The lights dimmed slightly at the same hours each evening. He asked his father why certain things were no longer made, why some homes felt warmer than others.

His father answered truthfully but incompletely. Some things were harder to replace now. Making less was considered responsible.

He did not explain that responsibility had become a proxy for obedience, or that scarcity was being taught as virtue.

Over time, the absence itself stopped being discussed. It was folded into language, into expectation. People began explaining delays to one another before anyone asked. Apologies arrived preemptively. Wanting too much started to sound childish, long before it wasn't even an option.

Once scarcity had been normalized, attention turned to what people did with what remained.

Recreational gardening changed tone before it changed status.

Articles appeared discussing inefficiency, water misuse, aesthetic inconsistency. The language was neutral, technical, disinterested. The condemnation was not overt; it was contextualized. It became something people joked about giving up, the way one jokes about habits they already intend to abandon.

Some neighbors stopped planting on their own, letting the work of the past wilt away without second thought. Others actively reduced their plots. Those who continued noticed inconveniences so minor they were unable to initially understand the cause. Utilities that flickered. Pressure drops. Inspections that took longer than necessary. None of it was punitive enough to protest. All of it was irritating enough to reconsider.

When the ban finally came, it used the same language as the mining suspension. Temporary measures. Restriction to restructure. Environmental mismanagement.

By then, most people had already complied.

The problems did not stop for the holdouts after they did.

Ulmus's father watched a neighbor dismantle his last soil beds, boxing the dirt carefully, like something fragile that no longer belonged outdoors. They did not speak about it. Weeks later, that same neighbor pressed something small into his hand without explanation. A seed, wrapped carefully. Not for planting any time soon.

That night, Ulmus's father understood something that frightened him more than loss.

Inheritance had become symbolic.

What he could give his son would not survive inspection, confiscation, or time. It would survive only by being unnoticed.

He accepted then, that whatever Ulmus inherited from him, he would pay for himself.

Everyone paid for what they received; what they gave was never guaranteed an equal return.

Opt-in benefits. Faster queues. Warmer housing. Priority access.

No penalties for abstention. Just acceleration for alignment.

They adjusted their language. Their posture. Their habits.

Ulmus noticed.

A neighbor's child received new shoes. Another family's apartment grew brighter, warmer. Celebrities spoke casually about personal optimization. Thin is in, they said, smiling. Nicotine was reframed. Focus aid. Appetite regulation. A clean choice. Cartoon characters chanting about "A leaner world is a cleaner world."

One family down the street began using nicotine pouches together. Uniformly. Publicly. Within weeks, their access improved.

Ulmus asked why they did not do the same.

His father felt the question land where it was designed to.

"It costs more than it looks like," he said.

That was all.

Ulmus tried the pouches later, influenced by proximity and an unsatisfactory answer. His father noticed and did not react immediately. He calculated the cost of intervention versus withdrawal. Opting in was not the danger. Opting out was.

He said nothing. He absorbed it.

He began to teach different lessons.

How to be quiet without being invisible. How to wait without appearing resistant. How to hold something without showing it.

He took the stress into himself and let his son keep wonder. The weight bent him slowly.

Language began overwriting memory.

Ulmus forgot things his father had never explicitly taught. Words replaced sensations. Descriptions displaced experience.

Stories could no longer be told whole. They had to be reduced.

Compressed into objects. Symbols that could pass unnoticed.

The seed became one of these.

Ulmus's father did not give it to his son. He gave it to someone who understood waiting. He asked him to hide it until the right time. He did not explain what the right time would look like.

He understood the risk. The seed might save his son. It might kill him. It would outlive his explanations. What survived would do so without him.

About the Author

Zakariyas James got his start writing self-published observational essays and has now branched into the art of storytelling with his fictional debut, Canopy. His works, both fiction and nonfiction, explore human behavior and their often unseen influences. He has a passion for understanding history, and his perspective on how our present world came to be and possibly where it could go next, can be seen throughout his writing.

Zakariyas lives in Florida with his wife and their 1-year-old son. With a background in music composition, he enjoys making music when not reading or writing. In his free time, Zakariyas likes to spend time with his family and loves to go to Costco for a $1.50 hotdog.

To connect with Zakariyas and view his nonfiction works, visit his blog, The Rumination Compilation.

www.ingramcontent.com/pod-product-compliance
Lightning Source LLC
LaVergne TN
LVHW092101060526
838201LV00047B/1504